For Bryan, Kelly, Danny, and Light Catchers everywhere
—Courtney

For my family, who fight for light, peace, and love; always
—Natalie

Published by Orange Hat Publishing 2018

ISBN 978-1-948365-25-3 Hardcover
ISBN 978-1-948365-28-4 Paperback
Library of Congress Control Number: 2018941909

Addision the Light Catcher
Written by courtney kotloski
Illustrated by natalie sorrentino

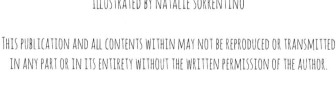
Orange Hat
PUBLISHING

www.orangehatpublishing.com

Addison the Light Catcher

The Gnat & Corky Series

Written by courtney kotloski
Illustrated by natalie sorrentino

Did you know there is light inside of everyone?

There is.

And did you know you can catch it
and share it with the world?

You can.

This is my super-duper light catcher;
it's fast, dependable and sparkly.

I made it when my brother was born, because when he opened his eyes the light was jumping around everywhere.

At first, it hit me right in the eye, and bounced off the nursery wall out into the hallway. I told it to stop,

but the light just kept running.

I chased it around the house,
through the laundry room,
across the living room,
past the kitchen,

and out the front door.

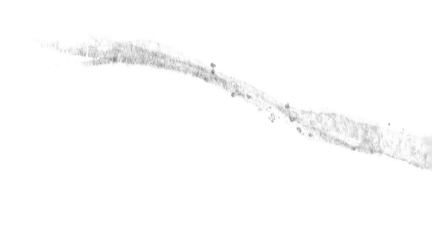

It stood shaking by the mailbox and I tried to plead with it.

"Please, light! Let me catch you. I'll put you up in the sky for all the world to see!" But the light just kept on running.

Through the garden,

out past the barn,

and into the woods until finally we both had to
stop because we could hardly breathe.

"Please, light. Listen to me.
I'll take care of you and
put you in a place where
all the world can see how
beautiful and special
you are to me."

The light blinked and
moved from side to side
trying to decide if it
trusted me.
I realized it was afraid
of what the world
might think.

I moved closer and gently held
out my hand.
"The world needs your light and I
can help you shine."
I cupped my hands together and
invited the light in.
Then slowly, with a trusting sigh,
the light surrendered and poured
into my hands.

That's when I made my wish...
"I wish I may,
I wish I might,
be forever the keeper of
my brother's light!"

I stretched my arm back as far
as it could go, and tossed the
light up towards the stars with
all my might.
The light looked down smiling
and beautiful from its place
in the sky.
It twinkled, and sparkled,
and danced in my eyes.

There it stands night after
night and day after day,
the brightest light I've ever
been lucky enough to catch ...

My brother's.

Sool Shine

Meet Addison and Asher

The world is a better place because of big
sisters like Addison. She is her brother
Asher's biggest advocate, best friend,
and a bright light for all children with
Down syndrome and special needs. At the
young age of eight, Addison understands
what is most important: love, acceptance
and happiness. If you live your life like
Addison, you can add magic to the world in
ways you have never imagined.

Hey, kids!

Visit www.gnatandcorky.com and answer our questions. You could be the next Gnat & Corky story.

CPSIA information can be obtained
at www.ICGtesting.com
Printed in the USA
LVHW07n1707080718
583080LV00012B/77/P